CHARLIE McGREW
& the Horse That He Drew

Written and illustrated by

Rob Biddulph

This book belongs to:

Jemimah

I am a reader and I celebrated World Book Day 2024 with this gift
from my local bookseller and HarperCollins *Children's Books*.

World Book Day

World Book Day's mission is to offer every child and young person the opportunity
to read and love books by giving you the chance to have a book of your own.

To find out more, and for fun activities including video stories, audiobooks and
book recommendations, visit **worldbookday.com**

World Book Day is a charity sponsored by National Book Tokens.
World Book Day® and the associated logo are the registered trademarks of **World Book Day**® **Limited**.
Registered charity number 1079257 (England and Wales). Registered company number 03783095 (UK).

HarperCollins *Children's Books*

KEEP AN EYE
OUT FOR THIS
PENCIL

This is the story of Charlie McGrew,
A regular, art-loving kid, just like you.

He
lives
in
a
flat
on
the

17th
floor

With a sign
that says

SORRY,
NO PETS

on the door.

ADD THE
OTHER
RESIDENTS

Oh, what he would give
for a doggy like Pat's.

Or Kylie's chinchilla.

Or Lorelei's cats.

Alas, that can't happen.
NO PETS the sign said.

So Charlie's decided
to *draw* one instead.

He starts with a head
and two ears at the top.

A body...

plus hooves
that go clippety-clop...

A long,
swishy
tail...

and a nice pair of eyes...

The boy greets the horse with a friendly embrace.
"Hello! Nice to meet you. But... why the long face?

"Oh dear. Are you hungry? Would you like some lunch?"
Let's draw this horse something delicious to munch.

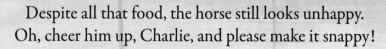

Despite all that food, the horse still looks unhappy.
Oh, cheer him up, Charlie, and please make it snappy!

"I've got it!" says C with a confident grin.
"This horsey wants someone to colour him in!"

GIVE THE HORSE SOME LOVELY BRIGHT COLOURS

That colour is fab, but the horse still looks glum.
What else can we draw to help cheer up our chum?

A HAT...

Bunch of FLOWERS...

ADD SOME MORE FLOWERS

A SPORTS CAR...

ADD SOME COLOUR TO THE CAR

72

NEW shoes.

But still this poor horse has a case of the blues.

Then all of a sudden
a lightbulb appears –

The penny has dropped
and the mystery clears.

A confident Charlie stands up, straight and tall:
"I don't think this horsey's a horsey at all!"

ADD A HORN
TO THE HORSE'S
FOREHEAD

He then,
with his pen,
draws a
magical horn...

Everyone smiles at our heroes ascending.
I do love a book with a nice happy ending.

Look out for more books by Rob Biddulph

5 things to find in this book

1 A BEARDED PIRATE ☐

2 A MOUSE IN HIDING ☐

3 A PET ALLIGATOR ☐

4 A BLUE NOTEPAD ☐

5 A RED KITE ☐